RUDY ROCKS

GRATITUDE

Text Copyright © 2012 Cindy Finley
Illustrations Copyright © 2012 Jamie Morgan-Finley
Editor- Genise Giarratano-Finley

Teach our children how to carry the coin with them during the day and use it to remind
them to be grateful for the people and things they have in their life. Hold it in your hand
and say "Thank You, Thank You, Thank You" for something in your life. We need to
learn to say "Thank You" several times a day starting early in the morning, throughout the
day, and before we go to bed. Rudy's message is to live with an **Attitude of Gratitude!**

Keep charging down the gratitude path for more adventures
with Rudy and his latest books, lessons, products and
FREE Newsletter. To learn more about Rudy's Gratitude
products visit
www.rhinotude.com or www.gratitudepathbooks.com.

A letter from Ms. Zana and her preschool students in Florida.

Dear Ms. Cindy and Ms. Jamie,
Thank you for giving us the books about the Zebra and Rhino. We like how Zoe the Zebra learned to give toys to other friends that live in the jungle. Rudy the Rhino taught Zoe the Zebra how to give.
We love the book and the pictures. Please make another book.

Current Books from Rudy...

Zoë Zebra Learns About Giving

Future Books from Rudy...

Gina Giraffe Learns About Helping
Gomer Gorilla Learns About Bullying
Elle Elephant Learns about Earning, Saving, and Spending Money
Alex Alligator Learns About the 'Law of Attraction'

Rudy Rhino and Lance Lion were walking down the jungle path on their way to school.

Rudy said to Lance, "I'm excited about our first day at school." "Me too!" said Lance, "I can't wait until lunch time."

Gratitude
Elementary
School

On the first day of school Rudy and Lance
were eating lunch in the cafeteria.

As Rudy and Lance were enjoying their lunch, Rudy noticed a new student sitting by himself at a table without anything to eat.

Rudy said to Lance, "Let's go over and sit by the new student." Lance agreed, so they both went to sit by him.

"Hi, my name is Rudy and this is my friend
Lance." "Hi, I'm Herbie Hippo. I'm a new student here
at school."

Rudy asked Herbie, "May we sit with you for lunch?"
Herbie said, "Sure, I would like that!"

Rudy asked Herbie, "Where is your lunch?" Herbie told Rudy and Lance, "I was nervous about my first day of school and left my lunch at home."

12

"That's no problem!" Rudy said. "My mom packed a big lunch and I'll share some of it with you." Herbie thanked him.

Lance said to Herbie, "You can have some of my
lunch also!"

This put a big smile on Herbie's face. Herbie said, "Gee, thank you for sharing!"

Rudy, Lance, and Herbie enjoyed the rest of their lunch period eating and talking.

After lunch, Rudy, Lance, and Herbie went to the school playground to play soccer.

24

While playing soccer, Lance said to Rudy, "Herbie is cool. I'm glad we shared our lunch with him."

Rudy was happy, knowing that Lance and Herbie learned about sharing with others.

From that day on, Rudy, Lance, and Herbie were best friends.

Best friends...walking down the gratitude path.

GRATITUDE AROUND THE WORLD

Visit www.rhinotude.com to purchase Rudy's products...

Gratitude Coin
Gratitude Bracelet
Youth and Adult T-shirts

Cindy Finley (right) was born in Gary, Indiana. She has been teaching at the preschool and elementary school levels since 1990. Based on her years of experience, Cindy identified the need to teach children fundamental lessons using gratitude as the core element. She believes that the fast pace of present day technologies and over-regulated standards of learning instruction have created and 'educational void' in children's lives. Cindy has recognized an improvement in the learning process when adults spend quality time with children using gratitude as the fundamental building block to motivate and enhance learning habits and skills. She has initiated a mission through Rudy's series of lessons on gratitude to reach out and teach children and adults how to make substantial improvements in life with simple and easy to understand lessons. Cindy challenges all adults to spend time teaching our children about the values and benefits of using gratitude on a daily basis. Cindy's goal is to establish Rudy as a household name and the ambassador of gratitude to the world.

Jamie Morgan-Finley (left) was born in Radford, Virginia. She is a graduate of the Art Institutes of America in Charlotte, North Carolina. Jamie's passion for the Arts, mixed with her enthusiasm to teach children, and working with Cindy, led to the creation of Rudy the Rhino and his jungle friends. Jamie used her brilliant artistic talents to create characters and a picture book environment that helps teach stories in a way that children can understand and follow simple lessons based on the idea of gratitude. She has created caring and loving characters that children can relate to; delivering basic fundamental needs to our children in today's social climate. Jamie's art work not only appears in Rudy's book series, but her designs are used on Rudy's gratitude T-shirts and challenge coins.